For Eleanor,
seven pounds, one ounce

First published 2020 by Walker Books Ltd
87 Vauxhall Walk, London SE11 5HJ

This edition published 2022

10 9 8 7 6 5 4 3 2 1

© 2020 Blackbird Design Pty Ltd

The right of Bob Graham to be identified as author of this work has been
asserted in accordance with the Copyright, Designs and Patents Act 1988

Printed in China

British Library Cataloguing in Publication Data:
a catalogue record for this book is available from the British Library

ISBN 978-1-5295-0405-7

www.walker.co.uk

This Walker book belongs to:

**The item should be returned or renewed
by the last date stamped below.**

Dylid dychwelyd neu adnewyddu'r eitem erbyn
y dyddiad olaf sydd wedi'i stampio isod.

To renew visit / Adnewyddwch ar
www.newport.gov.uk/libraries

Ellie's Dragon

BOB GRAHAM

WALKER BOOKS

AND SUBSIDIARIES

LONDON • BOSTON • SYDNEY • AUCKLAND

When Ellie was quite young, she found a newborn dragon.
With its eyes not yet open, it crawled across an egg box.
It was pale and luminous with shifting
rainbow colours, like oil on water.

Its little claws tickled in the palm of her hand.
It was quite the sweetest thing she had ever seen.

She called
him Scratch.

At home, she made him a bed.
Scratch opened his eyes,
black as charcoal.

His tiny wings shivered; he was flightless as a silkworm.

"He wants some matches, Mummy.
He wants to eat the tops off."

"Certainly not!" replied her mum.
"You can't play with matches, sweetie."

Her mum saw nothing but an empty
matchbox and cotton wool.

For a time, Scratch lived on the first floor of Ellie's dollhouse. She trained him to use the box of dragon litter. Ellie fed her beast nasturtiums, chillies and burnt toast, with barbecue coals for mains.

Ellie grew a little and went to nursery.

Ali saw him.

"He's sweet," he said.

Angie saw him, too.

"He's gorgeous," she said.

"Cool!" added
Amber and Luke.

But the
teacher
saw nothing.

Ellie grew some more.

She turned five, and she started school.

She was so excited that she forgot to take Scratch along.

It clear slipped her mind!

So Ellie didn't see her dragon's first flight …

which was
mainly downward.

Ellie had her eighth birthday.

Ali, Angie and Luke were there.

While the candles were still smoking,

Scratch ate them.

And the same night, when all were asleep …

Scratch
flew!

Ellie's dad came to call for outings on the weekends.

He never knew he had an extra passenger …

or that Ellie shared her popcorn.

Two years later, on Ellie's tenth birthday,
Angie, Luke and Ali came for a sleepover.

But things were changing for Ellie and Scratch.

Ellie still loved her dragon.

But Scratch had way outgrown the dollhouse.

So had she.

Dragons breathe fire, dragons
breathe smoke, dragons fly.
Dragons don't dance.
Scratch spent more time
dreaming on his fire blanket
in the corner.

Then Ellie was eleven,
and Scratch began to fade.

With the boom-boom-boom of the
Disco Poppy Girls in her ears,
Ellie could no longer hear the slow pump
of air under Scratch's wings.

The year after,
Ellie could see right through him.

On her thirteenth birthday, Scratch's breath
barely melted the icing on the cake.
He didn't even eat the candles.

And then he slipped quietly away into the night.

Occasionally, Ellie thought to look
for him – and almost saw the flick
of a tail from the corner of her eye.

She thought she smelt smoke – or heard
a low fiery furnace over the fence.

But Scratch had not gone. Little Sam found
him wandering down the High Street –

a fully grown, house-trained, affectionate dragon,
just looking for a new home.

And Scratch will probably live
with him for some time to come.

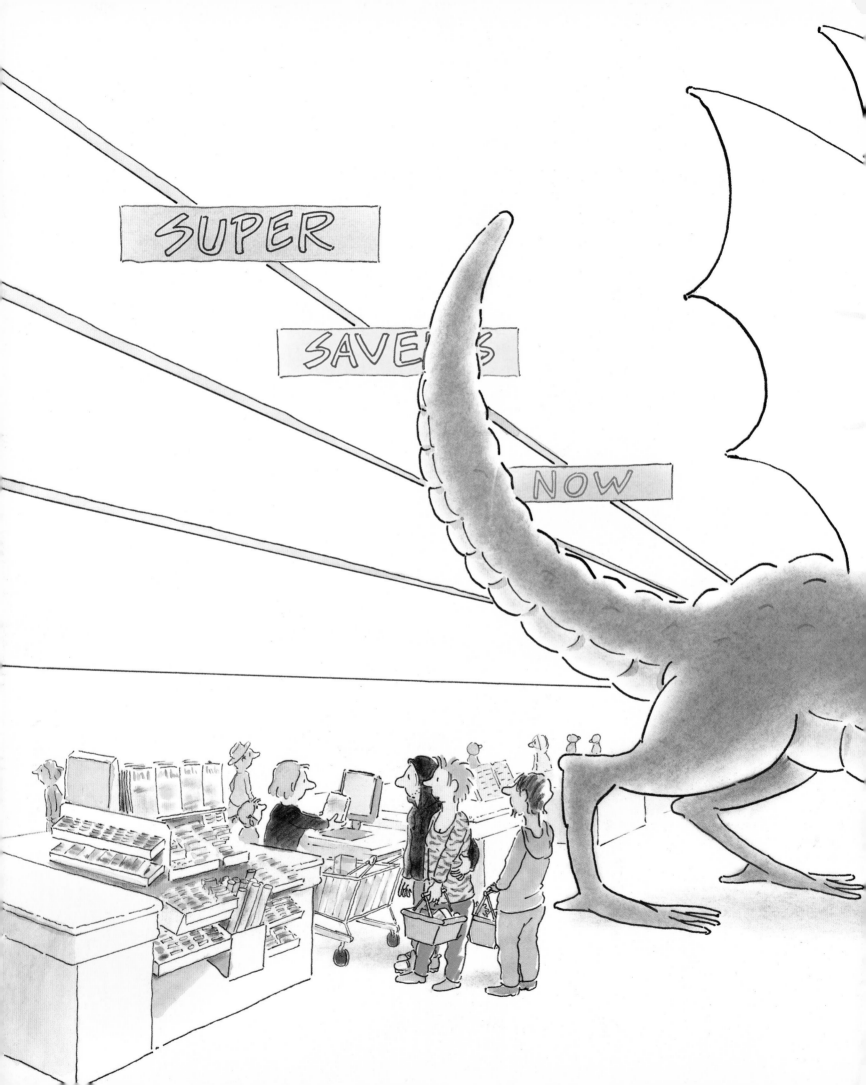

Bob Graham is a Kate Greenaway-winning bookmaker who has written and illustrated many acclaimed children's picture books including *Max*, *Maxine*, *The Poesy Ring*, *Home in the Rain*, *How to Heal a Broken Wing*, *How the Sun Got to Coco's House*, *April Underhill, Tooth Fairy* and *The Underhills, A Tooth Fairy Story*. His 2011 title, *A Bus Called Heaven*, is endorsed by Amnesty International UK and was the winner of the 2012 Children's Book Council of Australia Picture Book of the Year Award – a prize Bob has won an unprecedented seven times. He has been awarded the prestigious Prime Minister's Literary Award in Australia twice, in 2014 for *Silver Buttons* and in 2017 for *Home in the Rain*. Bob lives in Melbourne, Australia.